BLUE-RIBBON HENRY

by **Mary Calhoun** ★ illustrated by **Erick Ingraham**

MORROW JUNIOR BOOKS
NEW YORK

To Anne and Hiram, good research sources for many of my books
—M.C.

Winning will eventually come to those who truly try.
This book is for those of you who never give up.
—E.I.

Watercolors over varnished pencil were used for the full-color illustrations.
The text type is 17-point Garamond Light.

Text copyright © 1999 by Mary Calhoun
Illustrations copyright © 1999 by Erick Ingraham

Published by Morrow Junior Books
a division of William Morrow and Company, Inc.
1350 Avenue of the Americas, New York, NY 10019
www.williammorrow.com

Printed in Hong Kong by South China Printing Company (1988) Ltd.

1 2 3 4 5 6 7 8 9 10

Library of Congress Cataloging-in-Publication Data
Calhoun, Mary.
Blue-ribbon Henry/by Mary Calhoun; illustrated by Erick Ingraham.
p. cm.
Summary: Although he feels insignificant next to the other animals
at the county fair, Henry the cat proves to be special in his own way.
ISBN 0-688-14674-0 (trade)—ISBN 0-688-14675-9 (library)
[1. Cats—Fiction.   2. Agricultural exhibitions—Fiction.]
I. Ingraham, Erick, ill. II. Title. PZ7.C1278B1
1999 [E]—dc21 97-6470 CIP AC

"Harvest, harvest, harvest home," sang The Woman.
In the back of the car were tomatoes, gladiolus, and a
turnip as big as The Man's head.

"Yowl!" Henry groaned. He was in the large wire cage, and that meant going to the veterinarian. The silly dog, Buttons, was with him.

"Yowl!" Henry said again.

"Wowl!" Buttons copied him.

The Kid laughed. "Not the vet—a *pet* show. We're going to the county fair. Maybe you'll win a blue ribbon, Henry. First place, best cat."

Henry's fur settled. Best cat, yes! He sang along with The Woman. "Yow meow, meow meow!"

They drove into the fairgrounds, where people thronged in the sun and dust. Henry twitched his nose at the smells of many animals.

At the exhibit hall the best of the summer's harvest was displayed for judging—vegetables, fruits, flowers, bales of hay. After setting their own produce on tables, the family went to find the small-animal barn.

"Meow," Henry protested, jouncing along in the cage. "Meow-ow-ow!"

"Enough yowling!" The Man opened the cage and took
Buttons by the leash. The Kid held Henry to his shoulder.

A 4-H girl called to The Kid, "Come see my pig! He won
a prize!"

They walked to an open shed with a roof and
stalls. "See?" The girl pointed to a huge pink mound.
Henry's head jerked. The mound had eyes.
"Squunk," it said.

"I've never seen a pig that big," said The Kid.

Henry had never seen *any* animal that big.

"Hey, that reminds me," The Kid said. "It's nearly time for the greased pig contest."

"First," said The Man, "we'd better put Buttons and Henry where they belong until the pet show."

At the small-animal barn there was a racket of dogs barking and chickens calling, "Ca-daw-cut."

"Yap-yap," Buttons joined in when The Man left him in a cage.

All sorts of animals were going to be judged during the show. A boy took his rabbit out of its cage for a very young girl to pet. Henry stared. What a big rabbit!

The pigs, the rabbit—all the big animals made Henry feel too little. How could he win anything? "Rowl," he muttered as The Kid put him into a cage. Even the cat next to him was bigger than he was.

"Snaa!" Henry told the cat, and curled up with his paw over his eyes.

"Now for the greased pigs!" The Kid hurried away with The Man and The Woman.

Later he woke to The Kid's shout of "Stop that pig!" He also heard sounds of animals squealing and children screaming.

Pig! Was The Kid fighting with one of those huge squunking animals? Save The Kid!

Henry had watched how The Kid fastened his cage door. Reaching a paw between the wires, he lifted the latch and butted open the door with his head. As Henry raced toward the noise, Buttons began to bark and jump against his cage door.

Outside, people crowded along a fence, but between legs Henry could see little pigs and children running in a mire of mud. Suddenly a pig lunged at The Kid, who slipped and fell. Henry darted under the fence.

"Yow!" He sprang at the squealing pig and chased it to the fence. Then he blocked it to give The Kid time to run away.

Instead, The Kid grabbed the muddy pig to his chest. "Thanks, Henry!"

The people at the fence were laughing. Someone called, "No fair, getting help from a cat!"

Nearby, a girl flopped on a pig. "Got him!" she cried.

Now Henry understood. The children were trying to catch the pigs. And everybody was laughing at him!

Henry ran. Away from the pigpen, away from the crowd. When he stopped, he didn't know where he was. But at least he wasn't where people were laughing at him.

Henry looked around. So this is what a county fair is—
so much to see!

He wandered past farm machinery, tables of wide-
brimmed hats and tall boots, a rack of dangling belts. He
watched a man with a painted face toss balls in the air.

"Kitty!" Suddenly a small child held a balloon toward
him.

Henry reached to bat it, but when his claw touched it,
the blowy thing popped. "Meowl!"

"Wah!"

As the little girl walked away crying, Henry recognized
her. She was the one petting the rabbit earlier.
But she was too young to be by herself.
Was she lost? He ran after the child.

"Look out, cat!"

Henry dodged out of the way of an enormous long-legged animal that clopped past him. A boy sat on top.

People's legs kept Henry from seeing where the little girl had gone. He was too small! If he were high on that animal, he'd be able to see.

Running after it, Henry called, "Yow meowl!" to the
boy.

"Stay out of here, kitty," the boy said. "The horses will
step on you." He rode into a field where more horses
cantered around in a circle.

Henry turned back. Where was the little lost child?

He heard music. Maybe she had followed the sound. He did—to a carnival. Then he spotted a great wheel that carried seats into the air. Just the thing to see where the little girl was!

Henry hopped onto an empty seat, and up he rose. Higher, higher than the trees. He could see all the fair spread out below. Over there was the muddy pigpen and the small-animal barn. Past some sheds and the table of hats.

As Henry's seat reached the top and started down, he saw the little girl. She was walking toward the field of horses. She could be stepped on—squashed!

"Yowl meowl!" Henry wailed, urging the Ferris wheel to bring him down.

At last Henry leaped to the ground and raced into the arena. He caught up with the child as she walked toward a trotting horse.

Henry darted between her and the horse, and the horse reared. The rider pulled the horse aside with the reins while Henry shoved the girl the other way.

Then, standing on his back legs, he pranced out the gate.

"Kitty." The little girl laughed, trying to pat him.

"Yow!"

She was following!

Past the sheds he coaxed her, past the hat table. When someone reached for the child, a man said, "No, let's see where the cat is taking her."

People began to follow them. Some were laughing, but Henry kept on, leading the girl toward the small-animal barn. And there in front was his family.

A woman ran over and threw her arms around the little girl. "Oh, honey, I couldn't find you!"

The Kid scooped up Henry and rubbed his head. "You cat! Lucky you came back just in time for the parade of pets."

Walk in front of the same crowd that had laughed at him at the pigpen? Meowl.

Music started to play, and the parade of pets began. First came a rooster marching ahead of a girl. Then some children carrying cages of chickens and rabbits.

Henry, Buttons, and The Kid followed the big cat.
Behind them was the little lost girl, who held a kitten.
As she and her mother passed the judges, the woman
stopped and spoke with them.

Goats, lambs, pigs—all types of animals walked in the
parade.

When it ended, the winners received ribbons. The big
cat won the blue ribbon for first place in the cat division.

"Mow," Henry moaned. He wasn't big and beautiful like that cat. Or cute like Buttons, who won a second-place red ribbon in the dog class. Henry wanted to go home.

But a judge was saying, "And one last award for a hero. For that child-saving, pig-catching, hind-leg-walking cat, Henry. Pet of the Show!"

"Henry, you did it!" The Kid exclaimed.

Henry felt a purr fill his chest. He stood tall on his back legs so the judge could hang the blue ribbon around his neck. And he stood even taller as he strutted back to The Kid, calling, "Yow meowl." Some smart cat!